MAKE More S'mores

Written by
CATHY BALLOU MEALEY

and Illustrated by
ARIEL LANDY

PUBLISHED BY SLEEPING BEAR PRESS™

Glowing coals are finally ready.
Roscoe holds his sharp stick steady.

Slowly turned and gently roasted,
Soon that fluffy puff is toasted.

Crispy grahams wait on a plate.
(Roscoe stacked them, nice and straight.)

He adds a creamy chocolate square . . .

"Is that for me?"
asks Grizzly Bear.

Roscoe shrugs,
"Bon appétit!"

Grizzly gulps the gooey treat.

"More?"
asks Grizzly.

"Sure, let's see . . .
One for you and one for me."

Roscoe, kind and gracious host,
Gets two marshmallows to roast,

Unwraps chocolate,
Sets up crackers...

"Hello!"

Uh oh!
Two more snackers.

Roscoe looks at Grizzly Bear.

Grizzly grumbles. "I can wait."

MUNCH! CRUNCH! SLURP!

Cubs lick the plate.

Roscoe hasn't had one bite.
Still, he's patient and polite.

"Will you stay? I'll make us s'more."
Roscoe counts: *one, two, three, four.*

Stacks the puffs onto his stick, but...

SNAP!

SPARK!

POOF!

They burn up quick.

"Whoops!
I need a branch that's stronger,
Not too dry, a little longer."

"Me, three!"

"Mama!"
Bears embrace with glee.

"What a party! Can I stay?
I will help if it's okay."

Grizzly groans. "Another guest?"
But Roscoe does not seem distressed.

"How nice of you to lend a hand!
This party's bigger than I'd planned.

Hold this plate?

Add some wood?"

"Roscoe, those smell really good!"

"Ready!"

Roscoe soon declares.
He shares the s'mores with all four bears.

Toasty,
creamy,
sweet and gooey.
Crispy,
crunchy,
slightly chewy.

Mama sighs. Grizzly grins.

"Yummy!" cheer the fuzzy twins.

Roscoe nibbles his last bite.
Yawns. It has been one long night.

He curls into a hollow stump,
A tired,
furry,
happy lump.

Grizzly tucks him in, "Sleep tight."
They leave a thank-you note in sight.

Roscoe snoozes, gently snores,

Stuffed with sweet dreams.
And s'mores.

For Liza and Ginger, who put up with my puns. Let's make s'more books!

—Cathy

☉

For Mom, thank you for sharing your love of nature, art, and all things sweet.

—Ariel

SLEEPING BEAR PRESS™

2395 South Huron Parkway, Suite 200
Ann Arbor, MI 48104
www.sleepingbearpress.com

Printed and bound in China.

10 9 8 7 6 5 4 3 2 1

Library of Congress Cataloging-in-Publication Data

Names: Mealey, Cathy Ballou, author. | Landy, Ariel, illustrator.
Title: Make more s'mores / written by Cathy Ballou Mealey and illustrated by Ariel Landy.
Other titles: Make more smores
Description: Ann Arbor, MI : Sleeping Bear Press, [2023] | Audience: Ages
4-8. | Summary: When Grizzly Bear shows up at his campfire unexpectedly,
Roscoe the raccoon graciously offers him a s'more, and when additional
hungry guests arrive, he happily makes s'more after s'more.
Identifiers: LCCN 2022037864 | ISBN 9781534111769 (hardcover)
Subjects: CYAC: Stories in rhyme. | Raccoon—Fiction. | Grizzly bear—Fiction.
| Bears—Fiction. | Animals—Fiction. | Hospitality—Fiction. | LCGFT: Animal fiction.
| Stories in rhyme. | Picture books.
Classification: LCC PZ8.3.M47 Mak 2023 | DDC [E]—dc23
LC record available at https://lccn.loc.gov/2022037864